W9-BDF-879

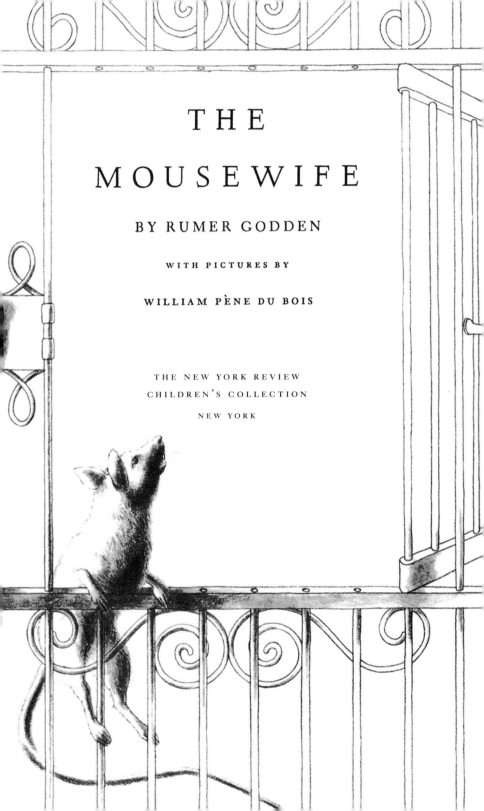

THE
MOUSEWIFE

BY RUMER GODDEN

WITH PICTURES BY

WILLIAM PÈNE DU BOIS

THE NEW YORK REVIEW
CHILDREN'S COLLECTION
NEW YORK

THIS IS A NEW YORK REVIEW BOOK
PUBLISHED BY THE NEW YORK REVIEW OF BOOKS
435 Hudson St., New York, NY 10014
www.nyrb.com

Copyright © 1967 by Rumer Godden, copyright renewed © 1995
Illustrations copyright © 1967 by William Pène du Bois
All rights reserved.

Library of Congress Cataloging-in-Publication Data
Godden, Rumer, 1907–1998.
The mousewife / by Rumer Godden ; illustrations by William Pène Du Bois.
p. cm. — (New York Review Children's Collection)
Summary: A house mouse who thinks there must be more to life than looking for
food and caring for her family befriends a lonely, caged dove.
ISBN 978-1-59017-310-7 (alk. paper)
[1. Mice—Fiction. 2. Pigeons—Fiction.] I. Du Bois, William Pène, 1916–1993, ill.
II. Title.
PZ7.G54Mj 2009
[Fic]—dc22

2008024715

ISBN 978-1-59017-310-7

Cover design by Louise Fili Ltd.

Printed in the United States of America on acid-free paper.

2 4 6 8 0 9 7 5 3

THE MOUSEWIFE

W herever there is an old house with wooden floors and beams and rafters and wooden stairs and wainscots and skirting boards and larders, there are mice. They creep out on the carpets for crumbs, they whisk in and out of their holes, they run in the wainscot and between the ceiling and the floors. There are no signposts because they know the way, and no milestones because no one is there to see how they run.

In the old nursery rhyme, when the cat went to see the queen, he caught a little mouse under her chair; that was long long ago and that queen was different from our queen, but the mouse was the same.

Mice have always been the same. There are no fashions in mice, they do not change. If a mouse could have a portrait painted of his great-great-grandfather, and *his* great-grandfather, it would be the portrait of a mouse today.

William Père du Bois

But once there was a little mousewife who was different from the rest.

She looked the same; she had the same ears and prick nose and whiskers and dewdrop eyes; the same little bones and grey fur; the same skinny paws and long skinny tail.

She did all the things a mousewife does: she made a nest for the mouse babies she hoped to have one day; she collected crumbs of food for her husband and herself; once she bit the tops off a whole bowl of crocuses; and she played with the other mice at midnight on the attic floor.

"What more do you want?" asked her husband.

She did not know what it was she wanted, but she wanted more.

The house where these mice lived belonged to a spinster lady called Miss Barbara Wilkinson. The mice thought the house was the whole world. The garden and the wood that lay round it were as far away to them as the stars are to you, but the mousewife used sometimes to creep up on the window sill and press her whiskers close against the pane.

In spring she saw snowdrops and appleblossom in the garden and bluebells in the wood; in summer there were roses; in autumn all the trees changed colour; and in winter they were bare until the snow came and they were white with snow.

The mousewife saw all these through the windowpane, but she did not know what they were.

She was a house mouse, not a garden mouse or a field mouse; she could not go outside.

"I think about cheese," said her husband. "Why don't you think about cheese?"

Then, at Christmas, he had an attack of indigestion through eating rich crumbs of Christmas cake. "There were currants in those crumbs," said the mousewife. "They have upset you. You must go to bed and be kept warm." She decided to move the mousehole to a space behind the fender where it was warm. She lined the new hole with tufts of carpet wool and put her husband to bed wrapped in a pattern of grey flannel that Miss Wilkinson's lazy maid, Flora, had left in the dustpan. "But I am grateful to Flora," said the mousewife's husband as he settled himself comfortably in bed.

Now the mousewife had to find all the food for the family in addition to keeping the hole swept and clean.

She had no time for thinking.

While she was busy, a boy brought a dove to Miss Wilkinson. He had caught it in the wood. It was a pretty thing, a turtledove. Miss Wilkinson put it in a cage on the ledge of her sitting-room window.

The cage was an elegant one; it had gilt bars and a door that opened if its catch were pressed down; there were small gilt trays for water and peas. Miss Wilkinson hung up a lump of sugar and a piece of fat. "There, you have everything you want," said Miss Barbara Wilkinson.

For a day or two the dove pecked at the bars and opened and shut its wings. Sometimes it called "Roo coo, roo coo;" then it was silent.

"Why won't it eat?" asked Miss Barbara Wilkinson. "Those are the very best peas."

A mouse family seldom has enough to eat. It is difficult to come by crumbs, especially in such a neat, tidy house as Miss Barbara Wilkinson's. It was the peas that first attracted the attention of the mousewife to the cage when at last she had time to go up on the window sill. "I have been running here and there and everywhere to get us food," she said, "not allowing myself to come up on to the window sill, and here are these fine white peas, not to mention this piece of fat." (She did not care for the sugar.)

She squeezed through the bars of the cage but, as she was taking the first pea from the tray, the dove moved its wings. I cannot tell you how quickly the mousewife pressed herself back through the bars and jumped down from the sill and ran across the floor and whisked into her hole. It was quicker than a cat can wink its eye. (She thought it was the cat.)

In spite of her great fright she could not help

thinking of those peas. She was very hungry. "I had better not go back," she said. "There is something dangerous there," but back she went the very next day.

Soon the dove grew quite used to the mousewife going in and out, and the mouse grew quite used to the dove.

"This is better," said Miss Barbara Wilkinson. "The dove is eating its peas," but, of course, he was not; it was the mouse.

The dove kept his wings folded. The mousewife thought him large and strange and ugly with the speckles on his breast and his fine down. (She thought of it as fur, not feathers.) He was not at all like a mouse; his voice was deep and soft, quite unlike hers, which was a small, high squeaking. Most strange of all, to her, was that he let her take his peas; when she offered them to him he turned his head aside on his breast.

"Then at least take a little water," begged the mousewife, but he said he did not like water. "Only dew, dew, dew," he said.

"What is dew?" asked the mousewife.

He could not tell her what dew was, but he told her how it shines on the leaves and grass in the early morning for doves to drink. That made him think of night in the woods and of how he and his mate would come down with the first light to walk on the wet earth and peck for food, and of how, then, they would fly over the fields to other woods farther away. He told this to the mousewife too.

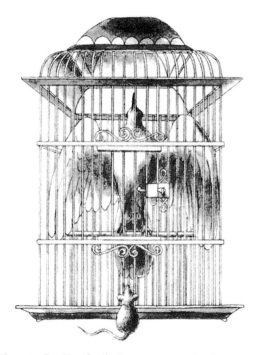

"What is fly?" asked the ignorant little mouse-wife.

"Don't you know?" asked the dove in surprise. He stretched out his wings and they hit the cage bars. Still he struggled to spread them, but the bars were too close, and he sank back on his perch and sank his head on his breast.

The mousewife was strangely moved but she did not know why.

Because he would not eat his peas she brought him crumbs of bread and, once, a preserved blackberry that had fallen from a tart. (But he would not eat the blackberry.) Every day he talked to her about the world outside the window.

He told her of roofs and the tops of trees and of the rounded shapes of hills and the flat look of fields and of the mountains far away. "But I have never flown as far as that," he said, and he was quiet. He was thinking now he never would.

To cheer him the mousewife asked him to tell her about the wind; she heard it in the house on stormy nights, shaking the doors and windows with more noise than all the mice put together. The dove told her how it blew in the cornfields, making patterns in the corn, and of how it made different sounds in the different sorts of trees, and of how it blew up the clouds and sent them across the sky.

He told her these things as a dove would see them, as it flew, and the mousewife, who was used

to creeping, felt her head growing as dizzy as if she were spinning on her tail, but all she said was, "Tell me more."

Each day the dove told her more. When she came he would lift his head and call to her, "Roo coo, roo coo," in his most gentle voice.

"Why do you spend so much time on the window sill?" asked her husband. "I do not like it. The proper place for a mousewife is in her hole or coming out for crumbs and frolic with me."

The mousewife did not answer. She looked far away.

Then, on a happy day, she had a nestful of baby mice. They were not as big as half your thumb, and they were pink and hairless, with pink shut eyes and little pink tails like threads. The mousewife loved them very much. The eldest, who was a girl, she called Flannelette, after the pattern of grey flannel. For several days she thought of nothing and no one else. She was also busy with her husband. His digestion was no better.

One afternoon he went over to the opposite wall to see a friend. He was well enough to do that, he said, but certainly not well enough to go out and look for crumbs. The mice-babies were asleep, the hole was quiet, and the mousewife began to think of the dove. Presently she tucked the nest up carefully and went up on the window sill to see him; also she was hungry and needed some peas.

What a state he was in! He was drooping and nearly exhausted because he had eaten scarcely anything while she had been away. He cowered over her with his wings and kissed her with his beak; she had not known his feathers were so soft or that his breast was so warm. "I thought you had gone, gone, gone," he said over and over again.

William Pène du Bois

"Tut! Tut!" said the mousewife. "A body has other things to do. I can't be always running off to you;" but, though she pretended to scold him, she had a tear at the end of her whisker for the poor dove. (Mouse tears look like millet seeds, which are the smallest seeds I know.)

She stayed a long time with the dove. When she went home, I am sorry to say, her husband bit her on the ear.

That night she lay awake thinking of the dove; mice stay up a great part of the night, but, towards dawn, they, too, curl into their beds and sleep. The mousewife could not sleep. She still thought of the dove. "I cannot visit him as much as I could wish," she said. "There is my husband, and he has never bitten me before. There are the children, and it is surprising how quickly crumbs are eaten up. And no one would believe how dirty a hole can get if it is not attended to every day. But that is not the worst of it. The dove should not be in that cage. It is thoughtless of Miss Barbara Wilkinson." She grew angry as she thought of it. "Not to be able to scamper about the floor! Not to be able to run in and out, or climb up the larder to get at the cheese! Not to flick in and out and to whisk and to feel how you run in your tail! To sit in the trap until your little bones are stiff and your whiskers grow stupid because there is nothing for them to smell or hear or see!" The mousewife could only think of it as a mouse, but she could feel as the dove could feel.

Her husband and Flannelette and the other children were breathing and squeaking happily in their sleep, but the mousewife could hear her heart beating; the beats were little, like the tick of a watch, but they felt loud and disturbing to her. "I cannot sleep," said the mousewife, and then, suddenly, she felt she must go then, that minute, to the dove. "It is too late. He will be asleep," she said, but still she felt she should go.

She crept from her bed and out of the hole onto the floor by the fender. It was bright moonlight, so bright that it made her blink. It was bright as day, but a strange day, that made her head swim

and her tail tremble. Her whiskers quivered this
way and that, but there was no one and nothing to
be seen; no sound, no movement anywhere.

She crept across the pattern of the carpet, stop-
ping here and there on a rose or a leaf or on the
scroll of the border. At last she reached the wall

and ran lightly up onto the window sill and looked
into the cage. In the moonlight she could see the
dove sleeping in his feathers, which were ruffled up
so that he looked plump and peaceful, but, as she
watched, he dreamed and called "roo coo" in his
sleep and shivered as if he moved. "He is dreaming
of scampering and running free," said the mousewife. "Poor thing! Poor dove!"

She looked out into the garden. It too was as bright as day, but the same strange day. She could see the tops of the trees in the wood, and she knew, all at once, that was where the dove should be, in the trees and the garden and the wood.

He called "roo coo" again in his sleep—and she saw that the window was open.

Her whiskers grew still and then they stiffened. She thought of the catch on the cage door. If the catch were pressed down, the door opened.

"I shall open it," said the mousewife. "I shall jump on it and hang from it and swing from it, and it will be pressed down; the door will open and the dove can come out. He can whisk quite out of sight. Miss Barbara Wilkinson will not be able to catch him."

She jumped at the cage and caught the catch in her strong little teeth and swung. The door sprang open, waking the dove.

He was startled and lifted his wings and they

hit hard against the cage so that it shivered and the mousewife was almost shaken off.

"Hurry! Hurry!" she said through her teeth.

In a heavy sidelong way he sidled to the door and stood there looking. The mousewife would have given him a push, but she was holding down the catch.

At the door of the cage the dove stretched his neck towards the open window. "Why does he not hurry?" thought the mousewife. "I cannot stay here much longer. My teeth are cracking."

He did not see her or look towards her; then— clap—he took her breath away so that she fell. He had opened his wings and flown straight out. For a moment he dipped as if he would fall, his wings were cramped, and then he moved them and lifted up and up and flew away across the tops of the trees.

The mousewife picked herself up and shook out her bones and her fur.

"So that is to fly," she said. "Now I know." She stood looking out of the window where the dove had gone.

"He has flown," she said. "Now there is no one to tell me about the hills and the corn and the clouds. I shall forget them. How shall I remember when there is no one to tell me and there are so many children and crumbs and bits of fluff to think of?" She had millet tears, not on her whiskers but in her eyes.

"Tut! tut!" said the mousewife and blinked them away. She looked out again and saw the stars.

It has been given to few mice to see the stars; so rare is it that the mousewife had not even heard of them, and when she saw them shining she thought at first they must be new brass buttons. Then she saw they were very far off, farther than the garden or the wood, beyond the farthest trees. "But not

too far for me to see," she said. She knew now that
they were not buttons but something far and big
and strange. "But not so strange to me," she said,
"for I have seen them. And I have seen them for

· 43 ·

myself," said the mousewife, "without the dove.
I can see for myself," said the mousewife, and
slowly, proudly, she walked back to bed.

She was back in the hole before her husband
waked up, and he did not know that she had been
away.

Miss Barbara Wilkinson was astonished to find
the cage empty next morning and the dove gone.
"Who could have let it out?" asked Miss Wilkinson. She suspected Flora and never knew that she
was looking at someone too large and that it was a
very small person indeed.

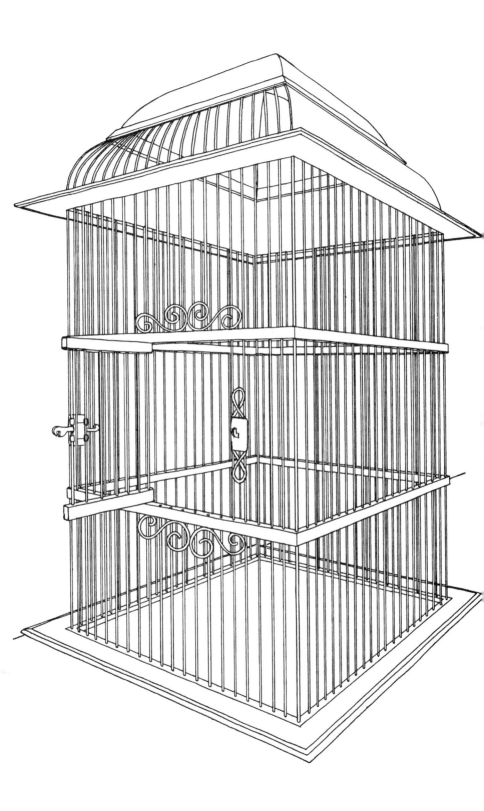

The mousewife is a very old lady mouse now. Her whiskers are grey and she cannot scamper any more; even her running is slow. But her great-great-grandchildren, the children of the children of the children of Flannelette and Flannelette's brothers and sisters, treat her with the utmost respect.

She is a little different from them, though she looks the same. I think she knows something they do not.

This story is taken from one written down in her journal by Dorothy Wordsworth for her brother William, the poet. It was quite true, but her mouse, I am sorry to say, did not let the dove out of its cage. I thought mine should, and she did.

R. G.

RUMER GODDEN (1907–1998) grew up in India, where her father ran a steamship company. When her husband left her penniless in Calcutta with two daughters to raise, she started to write books to pay off her many debts. She wrote over sixty books for adults and young adults, including *The Doll's House*, *Impunity Jane*, and *The Greengage Summer*.

WILLIAM PÈNE DU BOIS (1916–1993) was born in New Jersey to a family of artists and educated mostly in France. A founding editor of *The Paris Review*, Pène du Bois wrote some twenty-five books, many of which he also illustrated, including *The Twenty-One Balloons*, winner of the 1948 Newberry Medal.

TITLES IN THE NEW YORK REVIEW
CHILDREN'S COLLECTION

ESTHER AVERILL
Captains of the City Streets
The Hotel Cat
Jenny and the Cat Club
Jenny Goes to Sea
Jenny's Birthday Book
Jenny's Moonlight Adventure
The School for Cats

JAMES CLOYD BOWMAN *and* LAURA BANNON
Pecos Bill: The Greatest Cowboy of All Time

SHEILA BURNFORD
Bel Ria: Dog of War

DINO BUZZATI
The Bears' Famous Invasion of Sicily

INGRI *and* EDGAR PARIN D'AULAIRE
D'Aulaires' Book of Animals
D'Aulaires' Book of Norse Myths
D'Aulaires' Book of Trolls
Foxie: The Singing Dog
The Terrible Troll-Bird
Too Big
The Two Cars

EILÍS DILLON
The Island of Horses
The Lost Island

ELEANOR FARJEON
The Little Bookroom

PENELOPE FARMER
Charlotte Sometimes

RUMER GODDEN
An Episode of Sparrows
The Mousewife

LUCRETIA P. HALE
The Peterkin Papers

RUTH KRAUSS *and* MARC SIMONT
The Backward Day

MUNRO LEAF *and* ROBERT LAWSON
Wee Gillis

NORMAN LINDSAY
The Magic Pudding

ERIC LINKLATER
The Wind on the Moon

J. P. MARTIN *and* QUENTIN BLAKE
Uncle
Uncle Cleans Up

JOHN MASEFIELD
The Box of Delights
The Midnight Folk

E. NESBIT
The House of Arden

BARBARA SLEIGH
Carbonel: The King of the Cats
The Kingdom of Carbonel

JAMES THURBER *and* MARC SIMONT
The 13 Clocks
The Wonderful O

T. H. WHITE
Mistress Masham's Repose

REINER ZIMNIK
The Bear and the People
The Crane